The Book of Enoch

JANET HOWARD

Contents

Introduction

To everyone who will read the Book of Enoch and all the other books called "The Hidden Books":

These books were part of the Ethiopian Bible. In the 1700s, the Ethiopian Bible was brought into this country by a Freemason who was instructed never to expose these books or let them get out. They kept them hidden for centuries. Until 1948, the Book of Enoch and other biblical books were found along with the Dead Sea Scrolls. So, you see, Enoch was a prophet chosen by God.

I know they want you to believe that the Book of Enoch is just a myth or a story told long ago, but it is not. I will be writing to tell you the history of Enoch, his life, who he was to God and his family, and why the Book of Enoch was removed from the Bible.

The devil, the powers that be, the government, and those who run this country hide God's truth from us.

In the beginning of time, God created the world in six days and rested on the seventh day. God created man; Adam was the first man God created. Then he created woman (Eve), a helpmate for man. They had children, and their son Cain had a son named Enoch, after whom a city was named. But that Enoch was one of four mentioned in the Bible. We are talking about the Enoch who was seven generations down from the lineage of Adam, the Enoch who walked with God.

This Enoch wrote down everything that God's angels showed him—things that were not for his generation but for a time such as this. Enoch prophesied about what was written in the Bible, from the flood in Noah's time to the fall of the angels (Watchers) who had children with the daughters of God. These angels took the women on Earth, stole them from their husbands, and taught them how to make metal and jewelry, dyes, and how to perform all types of rituals.

Chapter 1:
The History of Enoch Family

Enoch's Family Bloodline - Genesis 5:1

Adam's descendants include two Enochs born into Adam's family bloodline. One was the son of Adam's son Cain, and the other was Jared's son. Jared was 162 years old when he had his son Enoch, as stated in Genesis 5:21. When Enoch was 65 years old, his son Methuselah was born. Enoch lived in a close relationship with God and would live to be 365 years old. When Methuselah was 187 years old, his son Lamech was born. When Lamech was 182 years old, his son Noah was born.

According to the book of Genesis, Methuselah was the son of Enoch, the father of Lamech, and the grandfather of Noah (referenced in 1 Chronicles and the Gospel of Luke). The descendants of Adam were Seth, Enosh, Kenan, Mahalalel, Jared, Enoch, Methuselah, Lamech, and Noah. The sons of Noah were Shem, Ham, and Japheth.

The Words from Moses from the Book of Deuteronomy 33:3

The Book of Enoch is not considered canonical by most churches, although it is by the Ethiopian Orthodox Church. The Book of Enoch, mainly in the Book of Watchers, dates from 300 BC, and the Book of Parables was composed at the end of the 1st century BC (1 Enoch 1:9). The pseudepigrapha is among the Dead Sea Scrolls (Colossians 1:16-18). Enoch spoke the prophecy of what would happen during Noah's time. Peter and Jude appear to quote the Book of Enoch in 2 Peter 2:4 and Jude 1:6. Both write about false teachers, referencing Genesis 6, which describes the sons of God as fallen angels, the daughters of men as human women, and the Nephilim as a race born from this union. In Enoch's story, God judges the fallen angels.

Enoch, the son of Jared and the father of Methuselah, is referenced in Genesis 5:21-22, Luke 3:37, Hebrews 11:5, and Jude 1:14. Do Peter and Jude actually quote 1 Enoch? Yes, they appear to quote 1 Enoch because they believed it to be true. They reference Isaiah 14:12-17 and Ezekiel 28:11-19, which refer to the fall of Satan. The Bible reads that Enoch walked with God, and he was no more because God took him (Genesis 5:21-24), which is interpreted as Enoch entering Heaven alive.

The New Testament has three references to Enoch from the lineage of Seth: Luke 3:37, Hebrews 11:5, and Jude 1:14-15. Matthew 19:28 asks, "What did Jesus say about Enoch?" Hebrews 11:5-6 says it was by faith that Enoch was taken up into Heaven without dying; he suddenly disappeared because God took him. Before he was taken up, he was known to be pleasing to God. Hebrews 11:6 adds, "It is impossible to please God without faith. Anyone who wants to come to Him must believe that there is a God and that He is a rewarder of those who sincerely seek Him." Hebrews 11:7 states that it was by faith that Noah built an ark to save his family from the flood. He obeyed God, who warned him about something that had never happened before. By his faith, he condemned the rest of the world and was made right in God's sight (Jude 1:14-15).

Summary of the Contents of the Book of Enoch

Jude 1:3-7

The Book of the Watchers tells the story of the fallen angels from Genesis 6:1-4. The fallen angels took wives, created the Nephilim— giants—and taught advanced technology to mankind, ultimately leading to the great flood and their destruction. We learn more about the functions of the holy angels in Heaven and about the great wars of the Nephilim, the men of renown from Genesis.

The Book of Similitudes is an apocalyptic book about the Son of Man, the Ancient of Days. These ancient prophecies of Jesus are directly in line with what we find in the Bible and are remarkably similar to the Book of Revelation.

The Book of Journeys reveals incredible insights about the afterlife, Heaven, and Hell. It poetically lays out the eternal fate of humanity and the meaning of the life of God.

The Book of Noah is the untold story of Noah from the Bible. We learn more about his mission to save all humanity and the struggles of his father Lamech and his grandfather Methuselah.

The Book of Luminaries is a detailed account of the stars and their functions. The imagery is similar to what we find in the Book of Job, where God presents creation and its mysteries to His servant Job.

The Book of Dreams and Visions is the prophecy of all human history, from the creation of mankind to the end of time and the final judgment. The past, present, and future are foretold in grand detail. The prophecy of weeks is similar to the prophecy and structure in the Book of Daniel.

The Epistle of Enoch reminds us how we should live. Enoch recounts the lessons and wisdom he has learned in life, and we are all subjects to God. Additional contents found in the MSV version of the Book of Enoch include ESV and ISV versions.

When did Enoch live?

Enoch, like Elijah, was taken to Heaven by God without dying in this life (Genesis 5:24 and Hebrews 11:5). The Book of Enoch was first discovered in Africa (Ethiopia) in the mid-1700s and also found among the Dead Sea Scrolls. Enoch, the grandfather of Noah, gave his writings to Methuselah, who passed them on to Noah to preserve them. These writings were meant to be delivered to this generation of the world. We should study and consider them as the word of God, just like the other major prophets.

I can't answer that question for you, but I have read it and found no contradictions in the Bible. In fact, many passages confirm and expand on what we have in the Bible. The prophecies are fascinating, such as the prophecy of the flood, which gives us a greater understanding of the world before the flood, and the ten-week prophecy, where each week is an era of 600-800 years. Since Enoch is mentioned several times in the Bible and was a man of God, and since the Book of Enoch was quoted by Jude and Peter, I tend to lean toward it being authentic and inspired by the Spirit like the rest of the Bible.

The Book of Enoch gives details about fallen angels (Genesis 6:4 and 2 Peter 2:4) and helps us understand where evil spirits come from. It also explains Hell much more fully. Sheol or Hades is a place of the dead, not just for the wicked but with several parts, including a good part for the righteous dead. In Enoch, Hell is described in greater detail.

The angels are called "watchers." Genesis 1:29-30 and Genesis 9:3 indicate that before the flood, everyone was vegetarian. After the flood, animals were killed for meat. Genesis 10:19 says God warned Noah of the deluge and assigned punishment to the angels who sinned. The Book of Enoch provides detailed information about these angels and their grievous punishment because they wronged mankind. The angels were bound for 70 generations until Judgment Day and the consummation.

The angels asked Enoch to petition God for them, but God denied their petition, telling them that they should intercede for men, not men for them. Their children would be confined to the earth as evil spirits since they were born of women and angels. The interesting thing is that the things they taught women were worthless mysteries and caused men and women to work, bringing much evil upon the earth.

The angels that sinned assumed many different forms. In the Book of Enoch 1:22, Hell is explained in greater detail than seen previously in the Bible. Tartaros is the deepest abyss of Hades, and Tartaroo is where the angels are reserved until Judgment Day (2 Peter 2:4). There are four different parts of Sheol where the souls of men are separated and reserved until Judgment Day (Chapter 70 in Enoch). Chapter 25:27 contains a prophecy of Jesus. John 4:24 says God is a spirit, and Jesus is human. Colossians 2:9, 2 Corinthians 4:4, Hebrews 1:3, and Colossians 1:15 describe Jesus as the invisible image of God.

Chapter 2:
The Epistle of Enoch

Prophecy of Enoch - Enoch 48, 1 Peter 1:20, Enoch 62: His name is revealed at the end and where he will sit. Enoch 69, Colossians 1:26, 1 Timothy 3:16: Enoch will sit on the throne of God.

Enoch 51, Chapter 55: In the last days, chapter 28, 36 Portal of Heaven chapter 32, showing us the Garden of Eden and telling a little bit about Adam and Eve. Chapter 36 ends the first vision, which started in chapter 1. Chapter 37-64: many visions, three parables, Luminaries, the portals of Heaven, and the stars. Chapter 48: The prophecy of the purpose of Christ since Abraham was not yet born. Chapter 51: The resurrection of the dead. Chapter 52: The Wrath of God. Chapter 53: The punishment of sinners and the righteous will have rest from the oppression of sinners.

Chapter 54: A deep valley for sinners, chains for the angels who sinned, a prophecy of the flood chambers of water above and fountains beneath the earth. Chapter 58: Promises to those who love the Lord. Chapter 60: A mighty quaking in the Heavens until this day lasted, the mercy and long-suffering of God, until the days of His wrath, Behemoth and Leviathan (these are not the same as in Job). Chapter 64: The angels who sinned, revealed what was hidden and seduced the children of man into committing sin. Chapters 65-70: Warning to Noah of the coming deluge and his preservation. The angels who were over the powers of the waters are told to hold them in check, to give Noah the teaching of all the secrets in the Book of Parables. The fallen angel Kasdeja taught men how to abort children in the womb. Enoch is translated to the place for the elect, where he saw the first fathers and the righteous who, from the beginning, dwell. Enoch was taken to the good part of Sheol, where the righteous are all resting and waiting for the day of the Lord.

Chapters 72-79: The Luminaries: the sun, the moon, stars, and the winds. The four-quarters of the earth. Enoch shows these things to his son Methuselah. Moonlight is transferred to him by the sun. Chapter 80-82: The sinners' years are shortened, probably referring to the lifespan of man after the flood being severely shortened to 120 years. All things on the earth shall alter after the flood: many things changed, animals, the climate, abundance of vegetation, etc. Sinners will be concerned with the stars. Enoch is told to declare everything to his son Methuselah to preserve it and deliver it to the generation of the world.

Chapters 85-90: The history of the world all the way through to the end into eternity. Chapter 85: Adam and Eve, Cain and Abel, Seth. Chapter 86: The fall of the angels who sinned. Chapter 88: The punishment of the angels who sinned, seized, and thrown into the abyss. The sons of the angels killed each other off. Chapter 89: The prophecy of the flood and the preservation of Noah's family - Abraham, Isaac, and Ishmael, Jacob and Esau, the family of Israel are created - Joseph, Moses - sin in the wilderness caused the current generations to be allowed to die without seeing the Promised Land, their children saw it. The judges: sometimes blinded, sometimes eyes open. David and Solomon: the kings, chronicles of the kings. The time of the rule of Babylon: the first 70 shepherds called, the rebuilders of Jerusalem, the second destruction of the temple and Jerusalem: the last 2,000 years and the wrath of God, Judgment Day, the time in eternity, and the New Jerusalem.

Chapters 91-92: Enoch tells Methuselah to call all his brothers together to speak to them, love uprightness and walk therein, and draw not nigh to uprightness with a double heart and associate not with those of a double heart. Chapter 93: The prophecy of weeks, the 10 weeks prophecy. There are some different theories about these prophecies. Some think it is 1,000 years for each week and that the first week is creation week and that the last week is in eternity, but that one does not fit all of the timelines and stated events well at all. It follows much more accurately that it is about 700 years for each week and each week might not be exactly 700 years, but each week is an era or period of time in the history of the world from creation through the millennial reign.

Chapter 3:
The Beginning of Creation (AA) After Adam

Week 1: Beginning of Creation, AA - After Adam

- *Enoch began to recount from the book and said, "I was born seventh in the first week, while judgment and righteousness still endured."

- Enoch's early years: he was the seventh from Adam.

- This was a peaceful era before the angels that sinned came to the earth. All creatures were herbivorous. The art of war was not known until the angels taught it to mankind.

Week 2: 700-1400 AA.

- "After me, there shall arise in the second week great weakness, and deceit shall have sprung up in it. There shall be the first end, and in it, a man shall be saved, and after, a law shall be made for the sinners."

- Great wickedness followed after the angels that sinned and came to the earth, taking human women for wives. They taught men and women many evil things, and mankind loved it and became wicked in their own hearts. When God decided to destroy the earth, it was because (Genesis 6:5) God saw that the wickedness of man was great in the earth and that every imagination of the thoughts of his heart was only evil continually.

- The first end is most likely referring to the first man, Adam, who died during this week.

- After this week, unrighteousness shall grow fully mature, and God makes a law of destruction for the sinners.

- Some say it was the translation of Enoch that was the man saved, but Enoch refers to himself in the 1st tense as I in the first person in the first-week prophecy, so he would continue in this one. Rather, it makes more sense that Noah was found righteous, before God, and, God declares the law of destruction for the sinners.

Week 3: 1400-2100 AA

- "And after that, in the third week at its close, a man shall be elected as the plant of righteous judgment, and his posterity shall become that plant of righteousness forevermore."

- *The flood happens in the first part, as well as the Tower of Babel and the dispersion of man around the world.

- *Abraham- believed God, and it was counted unto him for righteousness. God elects him as the father of the nations of Israel. It was the year 2046 AA when God made the promises to Abraham, and Isaac was born.

Week 4: 2100-2800 AA

- "And after that, in the fourth week, at its close, visions of the Holy and righteous shall be seen, and a law for all generations and an enclosure shall be made for them."

- Moses and the Exodus at the end, and the giving of the Law of Moses, the enclosure for them.

- Moses and the Exodus at the end, and the giving of the Law of Moses, the Mosaic Law.

- The Tabernacle and the Ark of the Covenant (the enclosure) are specified by God and created per His instructions.

Week 5: 2800-3500 AA, 500 BC to 200 AD.

- "And after that, in the fifth week, at its close, the house of glory and dominion shall be built forever."

- The time of David, Solomon, and the kings of Israel, Kings, and Chronicles.

- Some say this is the first temple being built in this time period.

- I personally think the house of David will stand forever, but the temple was destroyed.

Week 6: 3500-4200 AA, 200 AD to 900 AD.

- "And after that, in the sixth week, all who live in it shall be blinded, and the heart of all of them shall godlessly forsake wisdom, and in it, a man shall ascend, and at its close, the house of dominion shall be burnt with fire, and the whole race of the chosen root shall be dispersed."

- The blindness of the Pharisees and the proud hard hearts of Jews that Jesus spoke of during his ministry on this earth.

- Jesus was the first resurrection and ascension into Heaven and Hades.

- The second temple was destroyed during this week, and the Jews were dispersed among the nations of the world.

Week 7: 4200-4900 AA, 900-1600 AD.

- "And after that, in the seventh week, shall a prostate generation arise, and many shall be its deeds, and all its deeds shall be apostate, and at its close shall be elected the elect righteous of the eternal plant of righteousness, to receive sevenfold instruction concerning all His creation."

- Catholicism and Islam arose during this week, most certainly an apostate generation.

- Pagan rituals and beliefs mixed with Christianity by the Catholic Church, and Islam was a false religion that sprouted up.

- It was very hard to find anyone who truly loved God and was a true Christian during this time.

- It's hard to find any historical records around the year 900 AD that might be the elect righteous of the eternal plant of righteousness. Since all of the other significant events noted in the prophecies are about Israel and God's chosen people, it's safe to say that it is likely something we don't have a record of among the Jewish people or a heavenly event.

Week 8: 4900-5600 AA, 1600-2300 AD.

- "And after that, there shall be another, the eighth week, that of righteousness, and a sword shall be given to it, that a righteous judgment may be executed on the oppressors, and sinners shall be delivered into the hands of the righteous, and at its close they shall acquire houses through their righteousness, and a house shall be, built for the great King in glory forevermore shall look to the path of the uprightness."

- The righteousness of those who loved God and came out of the Catholic Church at the path of Reformation, men started looking to the path of the uprightness.

- The sword is two-fold: the crusades to stamp out Islam's rise and the Bible becoming available to man.

- At its close, increased and the saints of God multiply, God no longer dwells in houses made of hands, but dwells within His elect.

- The body of Christ, the saints, is the halo built for the great King, Jesus Christ.

Chapter 4:
The Book of Watchers, The Fallen Angels.

The Book of Enoch was considered a religious text. It tells us that Enoch was just a man who walked with God, and God opened his eyes to visions of in Heaven. The sons of God showed him these visions, and although Enoch saw and heard many things, they would not come to pass in his generation, but in a generation that had not yet come.

The first section of the book discusses the fallen angels (Noah and Noah's flood. According to the text, 199 fallen angels took human wives and had children with them—giants known as the Nephilim (Genesis 6:1-4). Semjaza, the leader of the fallen angels, led to the creation of the Nephilim, or Anakim giants, as mentioned in Genesis.

These angels taught humanity many things. Chiefly, Azazel taught men to make swords, knives, shields, breastplates, bracelets, and ornaments. Semjaza taught enchantment and root cutting, Armaros taught the resolving of enchantments, Baraqijal taught astrology, Kokabel taught about the constellations, Ezeqeel taught the knowledge of the clouds, Araqiel taught the signs of the sun, and Serial taught the phases of the moon.

Michael, Uriel, Raphael, and Gabriel appealed to God to judge the inhabitants of the world and the fallen angels. God sent Uriel is then sent by God to tell Noah of the coming cataclysm—the flood—and what he needed to do. God commanded Raphael to imprison Azazel and gave Gabriel instructions concerning the Nephilim and the imprisonment of the other fallen angels. The Lord also commanded Michael to bind all the fallen angels.

Enoch, the grandfather of Noah, provides unique material on the origins of demons and giants, why some angels fell from Heaven, an explanation of why the great flood was morally necessary, and a prophetic exposition of the thousand-year reign of the Messiah. It also describes the actions of Elijah the prophet in 1 Kings 17:2-24 and various tribes of the nations marching against Israel.

Two other books are named Enoch: Enoch 2, translated by R.H. Charles in 1896, and Enoch 3, surviving in Hebrew from the 5th and 6th centuries. Margaret Barker, in 2005, referred to these as "The Lost Prophet" in James Charlesworth's works.

The fallen angels were involved in mixed breeding with all of mankind, even animals.

Points of Interest:

The Antarctic - is a desert land with great frozen expanses, known as one of the driest locations on Earth.

Ten elongated skulls, ancient meteorites, fossils, 7 petrified remains of unusual animals, blood waterfalls, and dry valleys are found in Antarctica.

Rumors of the Lost Ark's presence in Ethiopia or Antarctica persist.

Genesis 5:18-24 outlines the genealogy of Enoch, who walked with God and was taken by Him.

Hebrews 11:5 speaks of Enoch's faith and how he was taken away by God, avoiding death.

Jude 1:14-15 refers to Enoch, quoting from the Book of Enoch, a book which is mentioned in Daniel 12:9-10 and 4 Ezra 14:44, where 94 books are referenced, 24 of which make up the Old Testament, and 70 were to be delivered only to the wise among the people Apocrypha. The hidden books.

Matthew 10:18 distinguishes between - books meant for public worship and apocryphal texts, which were too often reserved for use within the esoteric circles of the divinely-knit believers many of the critically spiritual or outside the realm of understanding themselves outside the realm of understanding and therefore came to apply the terms what they claimed to be Hectic work, which was forbidden to be read.

In 1773, rumors of a surviving copy of the Book of Enoch led Scottish explorer James Bruce to distant Ethiopia, where the book of Enoch had been preserved by the Ethiopian Church. In 1821, Dr. Richard Laurence, a Hebrew professor at Oxford, produced the first English translation, revealing the forbidden mysteries of Enoch. Eklelegmenos—the Elect One, meaning Jesus—is referenced in the Book of Enoch (Luke 9:35).

Three others that were named Enoch appear in the Bible: Enoch, the son of Cain (Genesis 4:17), the son of Midian (Genesis 25:4), and the son of Reuben (Genesis 46:9; Exodus 6:14). The latter two are transcribed as Hanoch in the modern translations, but the name is pronounced the same.

In the book of Daniel 12:9-10, (9) and he said go the way. Daniel 12:9-10 reveals that the books were sealed until the End time. Genesis 4:17 mentions that Cain's wife bore a son, and they named him Enoch, while Genesis 25:4 and Genesis 46:9 mention Hanoch, the son of Midian and Reuben, respectively.

Dr. Thomas J. Nettles explains that the Holy Spirit works through people in the Bible, guiding human writers to use their gifts in creating divine revelation. This process does not destroy the genuine personality and history of the writers, but rather, it shows how divine superintendence shapes human words into God's Word.

Chapter 5:
The Books That Were Sealed Until the End time

In 1773, James Bruce brought three copies of the Ethiopian Bible back to Europe and Britain after spending six years in Abyssinia. In 1821, Richard Laurence published the first English translation of these texts. The famous R.H. Charles edition followed in 1912.

There were 14 books known as "The Hidden Books" or "The Forbidden Books" of the Bible, which were removed by the Catholic Church. These books include:

- Books 1, 2 Esdras

- Tobit

- Judith

- The Continuation of Esther

- The Wisdom of Solomon

- Ecclesiasticus (also known as Sirach)

- Baruch

- The Epistle of Jeremiah

- The Gospel of Mary Magdalene

- The Gospel of Philip

- The Gospel of Thomas (The Twin)

- The Book of Enoch

- The Secret Book of James

- The Apocalypse of Paul, Letters of Peter and Philip

- The Apocalypse of Peter

- The Gospel of Truth

- The Gospel of the Egyptians and Judes

- The Gospel of Jude

Although I've listed more than 14 books, this is because some of the books that are still included in the Bible had certain teachings or some of the chapters removed. For example, not all chapters of Solomon, Paul, James, Peter, Jeremiah, Esther, and Ecclesiasticus were placed in the final compilation of the Bible.

The reasons for the removal or destruction of these books vary. Some scholars claimed that their doctrines were false or blasphemous and that these texts posed a threat to the Christian faith. However, this is not entirely true. The Book of Enoch, for instance, was written by the seventh patriarch from the Book of Genesis.

The lost books were not included in the Bible for several reasons:

They lack apostolic or prophetic authorship.

They were claimed not to be considered the Word of God.

These books were never authentically written by either Jewish prophets or Christian apostles.

In 1546, the Christian Apostles, the Roman Catholic Church have added certain books to the canon of scriptures in 1546 known as the Apocrypha, which means "hidden." The Apocrypha can still be found in the Eastern Orthodox Church and Oriental Orthodox Churches. The lost books of the Bible and the forgotten books of Eden are part of this collection.

The Matthew Bible, published in 1537, contained all the Apocrypha. The late King James Version (1611) placed the prayers of Manasseh after 2 Chronicles. The Apocrypha remained part of the King James Version for 274 years until it was removed in 1885 AD.

The Book of Enoch was accepted by the Ethiopian Bible, which consists of 81 books in the Old Testament, while the Orthodox Bible contains 51 books in the Old Testament. The Protestant Bible, in contrast, has only 39 books. The King James and the Catholic Bibles contain 46 books in the Old Testament, with an additional 27 books in the New Testament.

The search for non-canonical gospels or now-canonical writings can be done through resources like BibleGateway.com. Only the churches founded by the Reformers do not include these texts. The Orthodox Churches around the world, including the Ethiopian Church and the Coptic Church of Egypt, as well as the Eastern Churches in Iraq, Iran, and India, still include the Apocrypha, or hidden books, in their canon. The Protestants, while initially using these books, later sought to hide them from Christians and believers. The proper name of these is Deutero-Canonical books which means Secret canon or second list.

The proper name for these texts is "Deutero-Canonical Books," which means "second canon" or "second list."

The Apocrypha are religious texts that are included in some versions of the Catholic Bible, while others have omitted them. The word "apocrypha" comes from ancient Greek and means "those that were hidden." This term was first used in the 1147 editions of the Bible.

Chapter 6
The Book of Enoch - Question and Answers

Why should we stay away from the Book of Enoch?

It is said that the Book of Enoch is intended to distract from the truth. According to the Canon, Satan's plan is to divert attention from God's truth and make people believe it lacks power or is not true.

Why have churches tried to suppress the Book of Enoch?

Churches have attempted to suppress the Book of Enoch because the Bible references Enoch throughout the Old Testament. It also discusses the fallen angels and their giant offspring, who were destroyed during the flood. They did not want us to know the truth about the Book of Enoch, as it could undermine their control over us by keeping us ignorant about God's Word Apocryphal texts, including Enoch, were preserved by the Coptic Church. They believe that their versions of some texts, such as the Book of Enoch, were originally written in Ge'ez or Ethiopic—an African language—before being translated into Hebrew and Greek. However, these texts have been heavily tampered with. It is up to us to discern the truth. I am starting to think that the Book of Enoch should be considered alongside the Book of Revelation. Though most people do not read Revelation, I find it fascinating, full of prophecies, and thought-provoking.

Why is the Book of Enoch a book that churches do not want you to read?

The prophet Richard Laurence, echoing the days of Noah, claimed that Enoch said his writings were to be sealed and revealed in the last days. The Catholic Church initially included Enoch's writings in the Bible but later excluded them because they did not accept the idea that angels and human women had intercourse and created giants called Nephilim. Accepting this would require significant revisions to the Bible, as the truth can no longer be suppressed.

Questions and Answers People Want to Know

Why was the Book of Enoch forbidden?

The Book of Enoch was rejected by the Jewish community because it contained prophecies about the coming of Jesus Christ. They denied its canonicity and considered The Epistle of Jude uncanonical because it references an Apocryphal work.

In Hebrews 11:5, it says, "By faith Enoch was translated to Heaven so that he did not see death. He had this testimony that he pleased God."

What does the Book of Enoch say about Nephilim?

In Jubilees 7:21-25, Enoch describes the Nephilim as evil giants with evil spirits, stating that one of God's purposes for the flood was to rid the earth of these Nephilim.

Why were the hidden books left out of the Bible?

These texts were known to only a few people or were excluded because they were written at a later date and, therefore, not included. The Authorized King James Version refers to these books as The Apocrypha.

What does the Book of Enoch say about the Watchers?

In the Book of Enoch, the Watchers (Aramaic) are angels dispatched to Earth to observe humans. They soon began to lust after human women and, led by Samyaza, decided to take them as their own.

What does the Book of Enoch say about Heaven?

Enoch describes the Tenth Heaven. The first Heaven is just above the firmament (Genesis 1:6), where angels control atmospheric phenomena and storehouses of snow, rain, and water above. The second Heaven is a dark prison where rebel angels are tortured and where angels and demons reside. Azrael, the Death Angel, collects souls from here.

What are the three heavens?

The first Heaven is the reality we see with natural eyes, the place where we live. The second Heaven is where Satan's throne is and where fallen angels dwell in a dark realm. The third Heaven is where God has His throne or the Celestial Kingdom, where He rules and reigns over the universe (Genesis 28:12-16). 1 Kings 8:27-30 speaks about the spiritual realm and angelic travels. Satan visits Heaven twice. The third realm is the gateway to the heavens (Luke 10:16-18, Job 1:6-12). There are more levels or divisions of Heaven.

Which Bible has the Books of Enoch?

The Holy Bible King James 1601 version, The Apocrypha, and the Book of Enoch (paperback, April 7, 2017) is a reprint of the classic King James Version of the Holy Bible. It includes The Fall, The Apocrypha, and references from the Book of Jude. The Book of Enoch is included.

Who wrote the Book of Enoch?

Enoch is a prominent figure in Jewish and Christian traditions, considered the author of the Book of Enoch. He is also known as Enoch the Scribe of Judgment. The New Testament references Enoch three times from the lineage of Seth: Luke 3:37, Hebrews 11:5, and Jude 1:14-15.

Did King James remove books from the Bible?

It has been noted that the Apocrypha was included in every Christian Bible until 1828, when it was removed from some versions. The translators of the King James Bible argued that these books were meant to prepare people for the coming of Jesus, similar to John the Baptist. Yes, these books were removed. They were accepted for many years but later burned under the King James Bible's mistranslations.

Enoch wrote about the removal of his books in 1 Enoch 104:10-13 (RH Charles):

(10) "And now I know this mystery, that sinners will alter and pervert the word of righteousness in many ways, and will speak wicked words, lie, practice great deceit, and write books concerning their words."

(11) "But when they write down all my words truthfully in their languages and do not change or omit any of my words but write them all down truthfully—all that I first testified concerning them—"

(12) "Then, I know another mystery: books will be given to the righteous and wise to produce joy, righteousness, and much wisdom."

(13) "And to them, the books shall be given, and they shall believe them and rejoice over them. All the righteous who have learned from them all the paths of righteousness shall be rewarded."

My opinion is that they removed the books of Enoch because they did not want us to know about the different beings living on Earth. Now, with all types of aliens and different beings appearing today, it seems we are living as Enoch prophesied.

Who is the highest priest in the Bible?

Aaron was the first high priest mentioned in the Book of Exodus. Jewish traditions note that Enoch, succeeded by Methuselah, Lamech, Noah, Shem, Melchizedek, Abraham, Isaac, and Levi, were all high priests of Israel. Revelation 5:5 mentions the Lion of the Tribe of Judah, from which Jesus descends by lineage. Jesus is from the Tribe of Judah, as noted in Revelation 5:5 and the Apocalyptic version.

Chapter 7:
Quotes and Scriptures, Authors in the Bible who Spoke of Enoch Writing?

Authors in the Bible spoke of Enoch's writings, quoting scriptures and referring to various hidden or forbidden books. Out of all these books, Enoch was the most influential and frequently discussed. Most scholars date the books of Enoch to the second century BC. Enoch's influence began with the Jewish people in the first century BC and continued to be spoken about for 500 years.

The Ethiopian, Greek, Aramaic, and Semitic languages contributed to Enoch's texts. The book of Enoch was reportedly discovered in the 18th century. Enoch is also mentioned in the New Testament by Jude and quoted by Peter, both of whom were influenced by Enoch's writings.

In Jude 1:14-15, Jude mentions Enoch, who lived in the seventh generation after Adam, and prophesied about certain people. He said:

"(14) Listen, the Lord is coming with countless thousands of holy ones (15) to execute judgment on the people of this world! He will convict every person of this world who is living in sin."

Jude reminded the people that false teachers among them would suffer for their sinful lives. Peter also wrote to the churches about false teachers in 2 Peter, chapter 2, where the teachers were encouraging immoral lives. In 2 Peter 2:4-10, it states:

"(4) For God did not spare even the angels who sinned. He threw them into hell (Hades), in gloomy pits of darkness, where they are being held until the day of judgment. (5) And God did not spare the ancient world—except for Noah, who warned the world of God's righteous judgment. So, God protected Noah and his family when He destroyed the world of ungodly people with a vast flood. (6) Later, God condemned the cities of Sodom and Gomorrah and turned them into heaps of ashes. He made them examples of what will happen to ungodly people. (7) But God also rescued Lot out of Sodom because he was a righteous man, who was tormented in his soul by the wickedness he saw and heard day after day. (9) So you see, the Lord knows how to rescue His godly people from their trials, even while keeping the wicked under punishment until the day of final judgment. (10) He is especially hard on those who follow their own twisted sexual desires and who despise authority. These people are proud and arrogant, daring even to scoff at supernatural beings, without so much as trembling."

Jesus and his followers also quoted and were influenced by Enoch's teachings. Jesus studied the book of Enoch, which spoke of the Kingdom and the End Times. Enoch's books were sealed for 70 generations, and now, in our generation, these books are being revealed as God warns people of His coming judgment.

Here are some scriptures Jesus quoted that are similar to Enoch's teachings:

Jesus: "Blessed are the meek, for they shall inherit the earth." (Matthew 5:5)

Enoch: "And all the elect shall rejoice, and there shall be forgiveness of sins and mercy, peace, and joy. There shall be salvation for them, and a good light. But for all of you sinners, there shall be no salvation; instead, a curse shall abide upon you." (Enoch 5:7)

Jesus: "Woe to you who are rich, for you have received your consolation." (Luke 6:24)

Enoch: "Woe to you, you rich, for you have trusted in your riches, and from your riches shall you depart, because you have not remembered the Most High (God) in the days of your riches." (Enoch 94:8)

Jesus: "You also shall sit upon twelve thrones, judging the twelve tribes of Israel." (Matthew 19:28)

Enoch: "And I will bring out into shining light those who have loved my holy name, and I will seat each on the throne of his honor (glory)." (Enoch 108:12)

Jesus: "Woe to that man by whom the Son of Man is betrayed! It would have been better for him if he had not been born." (Matthew 26:24)

Enoch: "Where will there be a dwelling place for sinners, and where will there be a resting place for those who have denied the Lord of Spirits? It would have been better for them if they had not been born." (Enoch 38:2)

Jesus: "And besides, there is a great chasm separating us. No one can cross over to you from there." (Luke 16:26)

Enoch: "Then I asked, regarding all the hollow places (chasm), why is one separated from the other? (9) And he answered me and said, 'These three have been made that the spirits of the dead might be separated. Divisions have been made for the spirits of righteousness, in which there is a bright spring of water.'" (Enoch 22:9)

Jesus: "He will be great and will be called the Son of the Most High. The Lord God will give Him the throne of His father David (33), and

He will reign over the house of Jacob forever; His kingdom will never end." (Luke 1:32-33)

Enoch: "On that day, my elect ones shall sit on the throne of glory and shall try the works of the righteous, and their places of rest shall be." (Enoch 45:3)

Jesus: "That you may be called the children of the light." (John 12:36)

Enoch: "And now I will summon the spirits of the good who belong to the generation of light, and I will transform those who were born in darkness, who in the flesh were not rewarded with such honor as their faithfulness deserved." (Enoch 108:11)

Jesus: "The water that I shall give him shall become in him a well of water springing up into everlasting life." (John 4:14)

Enoch: "And in that place, I saw the spring of righteousness, which was inexhaustible. Around it were many springs of wisdom from which the thirsty drank and were filled. Their dwellings were with the righteous, holy, and elect." (Enoch 48:1)

Enoch spoke about the Elect One. The Hebrews and Israelites are called the Chosen People or the People of God (Chosen Ones). When Enoch spoke of the Elect Ones or Chosen Ones, he was speaking about Jesus. In Deuteronomy 7:6 and Luke 9:35, the chosen ones are referred to as God's chosen nation, Israel. Jesus, the Elect One, was whom Enoch referred to.

Luke spoke of the Chosen One, and Enoch referred to the Elect One, which is the same figure—Jesus. But we are also called God's chosen people. In Genesis, Abraham and his family were chosen. God's chosen nation is Israel. (Exodus 19:5-6) God chose many, including priests, Moses, and Abraham. He chose many to be blessed, but Israel was chosen for a purpose (John 8:12)—to spread the good news (Acts 1:5).

The Jewish people considered themselves God's chosen people. Enoch spoke of the Elect Ones fourteen times in the book of Enoch. "This is my Son, whom I am well pleased," was spoken when John the Baptist baptized Jesus. Enoch also wrote, "This is my Son, the Elect One, the one God promised," in the book of Enoch, and Luke also spoke of the Chosen One.

Chapter 8:
The Fall Of Babylon. Revelation 18;3.

The Fall of Babylon- America is what we call Babylon of Today, this is the time Enoch spoke about, This world system taught God's people lies, and is keeping them lost and confused.

The Elite and the Freemasons changed the bible and used it against God's chosen people, how they took our Land from us, used our ancestors(us) sold our children into slavery, and sexually abused Us.

Joel 3;1- 20. This chapter in the bible, The book of Joel Talks about the natural disasters that had and would take place, Where the would be suffering, Joel also speaks about plagues and locus This is how God is using these things to show us and warn us of the things that are coming.

God is warning us to stop sinning and turn back to him or they will suffer. There will be nothing we can do to stop what is coming, God will strip the Land Bare, with the Locusts and plague. Read Joel 1;4- 12 and in the book of Revelation 15, and 16.

The seven plagues that were described in Exodus 7;11. The plagues were water turning into blood, frogs, lice, diseased livestock, boils, hail, locusts, darkness on the Land for these days, and killings of the firstborn sons. All of the fruits on the trees will dry up, nothing will be left, nothing will be left, nothing to Eat. God will judge his Enemies, The Enemies of God are the people who scatter and oppress his chosen people (Israel). God is saying I will not let them get away with the Abuse, They have caused my people '' We must pray and turn back to God. We as a people must gather together, The Elders, children, and babies turn to God now, while there still time, give me your Hearts. God is calling the world to Repent. Joel 2;12, We must pray and cry out to God for God to spare us, In order for God to restore the Land and save us.

In Jeremiah 17;9,10 God speaks of the human heart,(9) The Human Heart is the most deceitful of all things and desperately wicked, who knows how bad it is? (10) But I the Lord search all Hearts and examine. Secrets motives. I give all people their due rewards according to what their actions deserve.

We Lose sight of what God had for us to do, one was to have no other God and to remember to keep the Sabbath day Holy.

God gave us the 10 commandments as Instructions on what we must do. Jeremiah 18;7-17 Read because we as people refuse to turn from the evil ways of this world, We will suffer despair and pain, We must Repent. Jeremiah 18;7-17 God says this is for my people who refuse to turn back to me. A message to Babylon. Jeremiah 51;14, We must prepare for war, tell my people the truth, I will protect them from their enemies, The ones Enoch speaks of these People (Scoffers). They followed their own natural Instincts, They Tried to Satisfy their own ungodly desires, and they did not have God's spirit in them.

Enoch lived in the 7th generation, after Adam, He prophesied about these people who lived an ungodly life. God will convict and bring judgment on all these people who have spoken against God. These people worshiped False gods and Ignored God's laws and commandments, which God placed in the bible for the people to live by(God's Chosen), Now today God is saying these things to us his chosen ones and The World.

God is giving us warnings to Judah in the Old Testament. People in this world today don't even want a relationship with God, but things will get progressively worse, because of the disobedience and because God never told his people to take on the ways of this world, but we disobeyed God and did them anyway. James 4;4-8, if we are a friend of the world, we are an enemy of God. 1 Corinthians 6;17,18, Come from among them. 1 John 2;15, Do not love the world or anything in the world. Isaiah 65;1-25 Please read this Chapter; it is important to the next chapter in the bible. Isaiah 65;12-15, (12) Now I will destine you for the sword all of you will bow down before the executioner, For when I called you did not answer when I spoke, you did not listen, you deliberately sinned- before my very eyes- and chosen to do what you know I despise. (13) Therefore this is what the sovereign Lord says' My servant will eat, but you will starve, My servant will drink, but you will be thirsty, My servant will Rejoice, but you will be sad and ashamed, My servant will sing for joy, but you will be sad and ashamed. (14) My servant will sing for joy, but you will cry in sorrow and despair. (15) Your name will be a curse word among my people for the Sovereign Lord will destroy you and will call his true servant by another name. We are still talking about The fall of Babylon, Revelations 18;2-6, the angels came down (2) He gave a mighty Shout' Babylon Is Fallen'- that great city has fallen! She has become a home for demons, She is a hideout for every foul spirit, a hideout for every foul vulture and every foul and dreadful animal. (3) For all the nations have fallen Because of the wine of her passionate Immorality. The king of the world has committed Adultery with her because of her desire for extravagant luxury. The merchants of this world have grown Rich. (4) Then I heard another voice calling from heaven' Come away from her, My people do not take part in her sins, or you will be punished with her. (5) For her sins are piled as high as

Heaven, and God remembers her evil deeds. (6) Do to her as she has done to others double penalty, for all her evil deeds.

God is still asking us to Repent, forgive, and turn back to him, Trust God - God said to the children of Israel, I took you out of Egypt now you are Trying return to go back into Slavery, Back to Egypt, Back to Babylon to Die.

Chapter 9:
The Book Of Insight, (Biblical History).

When I begin to search for a deeper understanding of the bible, I realize that I must search the History of the bible. I had to have a Theological, Social, and Historical understanding of the Old and New Testament. I had to answer questions like, when he was born, The family bloodline, starting with Adam and Eve, The Historical time in which they lived, and what prophecies, as I Learned about Enoch and some of his teachings were not placed in the bible, but removed as non-spiritual canon. The book of Enoch was in the Ethiopic bible as a Canon and also in the Roman Catholic Bible I began to question why people were trying to say that Enoch was just a story or a myth, but as I began to study the Book of Insight is what I call it because Enoch was mention at the beginning of the Bible, The history of Enoch. He was a true Prophet, and a scribe and he walked with angels and God took him so I guess you can say God really did speak to Enoch and Favored him. The 70 generation, which is now beginning to look like Enoch was really talking about the time we are living in, our time, about our end.

The book of Enoch, The book of Insight, The book of living.

 The fall of the angels and the fall of man, The fall of the Watchers, bringing conflict in the Heavens.

The Watchers-The fallen angels wanted to be human, Enoch was speaking about the fourth coming future, Enoch was speaking about the final generation.

The Angels- 70 generations - have no access to be granted, God would not let the fallen angels back into, Heaven.

Chartony-The devil's children, Enoch a reflection of the biblical story.

The history of the human race, Stars fallen angels, The book of Enoch speaks of the shapeshifters,(shapeshifting). 2 Corinthians 5, -2 Timothy - Mathews 24;32. The Secret of the Ancient black Indians, The biblical history reports that the Israelites were black and are still living in the Middle East.

Yahawehs- chosen people the true Jewish Israelites, Kus'sHe- means Nigga, Nogriod-means Black, The Israelites and the Egyptians were black.

ASHKENAZI- Jews of the European 11th century. Jesus was black, and Moses was black. Exodux 4- 2;15, Genesis 42, -10;1 son of Noah.

God is gathering his children back home, Isaiah 42.

The 12 lost Tribes of Israel, 12 tribes we must return to God's Laws by keeping the Sabbath day Holy, Deuteronomy 28;45, Zechariah 11;1, Isaiah 3;42-57-11;10 Blessing and curses.

Support of Israel-Jewish people, Ezekiel 22;23-31 Revelations 16;13,14, Isaiah 28;14-55.

Message to Babylon- America, God is warning us his chosen people to speak, The truth God said that he will protect all his people from your Enemies. Jeremiah 51;14. There is a book - The bible to understand the wars in Israel.

America-UTAH The book of Enoch, Babylon is America, The Promised Land Is Grand-Israel, The Jordan River, Mount Moriah.

The end prophecies, God has the final say in our lives, and God will not allow anyone to touch his chosen ones, his warriors.

The battle of Armageddon is coming, Enoch spoke of these people the Scoffers, people who followed their own natural Instincts, They Tried to satisfy their own ungodly desires, They did not have God's spirit in them.

The people who worshiped false gods and Ignored God's Laws and commandments, that God placed in the bible for them (Us) to live by, but today God is saying the same thing to us(The world) just like he Gave warning to Judah in the Old Testament. People in this world today do not even want a Relationship with God, but our situation will get Progressively worse Because of our disobedience God told us not to take on the ways of this world, but we disobeyed God anyway.

The High Priest Of Israel.

Jesus was from the tribe of Judah Matthews 1;1-6, Jesus in the NIV Luke #;31-34 as a member of the Tribe of Judah, the Lineage Revelation 5;5, mentions an Apocrypha Version of the Lion of the Tribe of Judah.

The High priest of God Enoch who was the first man considered a priest and those who succeeded him, were Methuselah, Lemech, Noah, Sham, Melchizedek, Abraham, Issac, and Levi and considered as high priest of Israel even though Arron was the first high priest mentioned in the book of Exodus in the Jewish, noted him as a legend as being the first man mention by the Jewish, but Enoch and his son and his grandson were also considered to be High priest.

Chapter 10:
The Nephilim Returning- The Fallen Angels.

The fallen angels, The Nephilim, are returning to the earth. In all types of evil in all forms, Aliens, two-body beings- man/ animal, fallen angels in human form.

The Nephilim are beings people mention in the Hebrew Bible, which are called giant beings, very strong and Tall. These Nephilim are sometimes called fallen ones or fallen angels and humans. These are the names that they are called or given, Angel-humans, Hybrids, or were called Nephilim, Goborim or Giants, Nephalem, even though the Nephilim are referred to as Angel-Human. Hybrids can be all other kinds of Half-Angels except The Nephalem, The book of Enoch, viewed them as offsprings of the descendants of Seth and Cain.

The Nephalem are more powerful than the Nephilim or Canbion.

A Nephalem is part Angel-Demon, Lilthand Inarius, where the firstborn Nephalem.

A Nephalem is a hybrid conceived from a demonic and a celestial creature, these beings are considered unholy beings and abominations of the multiverse, from a different place within the Universe.

Scientists believe that multiverse or Quantum mechanics say that the Universe we observe is just one of many or multiple dimensions, such as length, width, and height and also dimension of time. Nephilim Enoch is described as the son of God as be fallen angel.

The Nephilim the offsprings produced by human women, were mentioned by Enoch in a non-canonical Jewish text as female angels that had six wings, Seraphims described to have human heads and six wings, angels closest to God are said to be the highest sphere. They have eyes all over their wings. The Seraphim are described to have human heads and six wings, these angels closest to God are said to be the highest sphere and have eyes all over their wings.

What do the black angels represent black angels are fallen angels God vs the devil, The fallen angels Michael he is often described with black wings, and Lucifer is often depicted with white wings to describe his former state as an angel before his fall from grace.

Lucifer's real name is Semael is a fallen Archangel, who was banished from Heaven, By God after he failed he was rebellion, he was sent to hell as its new ruler, he later changed his name to Lucifer, and the angels who were thrown out of Heaven with him, Today Lucifer is known as Satan The chief devil, Enoch description of him as ruler governor (Prince) of this world, It was said that Enoch's transformation from a human being into an angel is the highest celestial Realm. Enoch is to be said to already be an angelic being.

2 Enoch 56 chapter 39-6 does Enoch become an angel?

God has withdrawn his protection and will allow the enemy, the devil to attack America this Land will be stripped of everything.

Demons and unclean spirits which are wicked, I'm not just talking about unclean spirits, but we are also talking about Aliens and the Nephilim spirits that are returning to Earth. This world which the government tried to hide and the fact that Aliens exist and the bible speaks of the Nephilim spirits. Ecclesiastes 3;16,17- 4;1-4.

Solomon spoke of evil in the courtroom. He said even the court is corrupt and God will judge everyone both good and Bad(evil). This is to let you know our Government is corrupt.

In this world, Innocent people often get hurt by the mistakes of others and their sins. In my book 'Trapped In A Pit With Generational Curses' I wrote about Ancestral sins.

Last going to write about the Cockatrice Spirit, a being produced out of the cock's eggs is the corruption of a crocodile-like Serpent., being a domonic Cockatrice spirit- Jezebel spirit-Leviathan divination, witchcraft, gossip, Slaider Perverseness, Jealousy, Envy, Sabotage Assassination scandals, Accusation-Absalom, injustice, Lying spirit, Covetousness, Deceiving and seducing Spirits and a Spirit of Offense, that just the Spirit of The Cockatrice. Now I'm going to give you the Description of the Corkatrice Being- That could kill a person with just a glance in a person's eyes. A monster part snake and part cock, It has a head and legs like cock, but a body like a Serpent and its wings, Isaiah 59;5,6.

When a person looks into the eyes of a person looks into the eyes of Cockatrice demons. They can not or will not see any truth in them, so some of these Cockatrices will take on Human form of Hybrid, like today they will celebrate wrongdoing and see nothing wrong doing and see nothing wrong and will not take on the ways of this world because this world is Corrupt and this world system is Corrupt, but we as the Righteous of God must prevail, God has place his chosen ones in this world to fight for his Kingdom.

The Cockatrice is an egg. It is a Mythical Hybrid a very poisonous Serpent that is about a footlong look like a dragon.

The Hebrews referred to it as (Tsepha), which is a nasty poisonous animal. The King James 1611 Bible Translated the word as Cockatrice, A Viper, I'm not too sure how this form of Hybrid can become Human unless it is better by one, I will just write about its looks, and about the behavior of this spirit, Not to go too deep off unto This being.

Chapter 11:
What Feeds the Behavior

Watch out for what feeds the behavior of others. It causes hurt, abuse, misunderstanding, and injustice that we suffer at the hands of those behaviors. Isaiah 10:27 says, "On that day, the Lord will end the bondage of His people. He will break the yoke of slavery and lift it from their shoulders."

To the children of Israel, God is saying, "I took you out of Egypt, yet now you want to return, to go back into slavery, back to Egypt and Babylon." The devil is at work in the hearts and minds of those who refuse to obey God.

We, as believers, used to live in sin like the rest of the world, obeying the devil (Satan), who is the commander of the power of the unseen world. Ephesians 6:12 speaks of this in the Bible. The body is a vessel, and it is up to a person what kind of spirit they will carry within them.

Ephesians 6:12 says, "For we wrestle not against flesh and blood, but against principalities, against the rulers of this world, against spiritual wickedness in high places." This brings me back to my first book, where I talk about spiritual rape. Spiritual rape is when a person allows certain influences to affect them, causing spiritual abuse. That's why I'm writing to tell people to be mindful of who and what they allow to feed (teach) their soul, because the opinions of others can be a form of witchcraft.

We must not, I repeat, we must not allow the opinions of others or unseen forces to stop us from moving forward in God. The purpose is the call that God has placed on our lives. I'm referring to the scripture,

"In times past, ye walked according to the prince of the powers of the air, the spirit that now works in the children of disobedience." (Ephesians 2:2)

In Ephesians 6:12, it speaks of the word "wiles," which means tricks intended to deceive, ensnare, or disarm. Wiles are seductive spirits or deceitful, cunning manners meant to fool or trap. These are the evil things done in a person's life by the devil, who attacks them physically, mentally, emotionally, and spiritually—sometimes even sexually. Only God can heal and restore a person.

We must humble ourselves and give our hearts to God. This is what I mean when I say we must repent and give our bodies back to God. If we do not return to God, we will continue to see more evil in the land as we live by the world's system.

God said, "If my people, who are called by my name, would humble themselves and pray and seek my face and turn from their wicked ways, then I will hear from heaven and I will forgive them of their sins and I will heal their land." (2 Chronicles 7:14)

We must emotionally and spiritually guard our hearts and souls. We must not leave doors open for the devil to enter our bodies. We must guard our hearts and souls by putting on the whole armor of God. Physically and mentally, a person must cover their heart (mind), because evil is at work in the unseen world and in people's bodies and minds.

We must be careful not to allow these spirits to take over or dwell in us, because there is an abuse of power in our government, politicians, and religion. Satan uses his power to try to control our bodies and minds. He looks for bodies to use, just like he uses Hollywood, our leaders, musicians, and actors—those who people look up to. People of influence are often the ones Satan targets. Evil spirits can only enter the body through sin (John 10:1-10).

Satan uses his power to try to destroy us—God's chosen people. The Bible tells us that the devil comes to kill, steal, and destroy, but God comes that we might have life, and that more abundantly (Ephesians 6:10-11).

The devil can enter a person's heart if they hold unforgiveness in it. This is what I mean when I talk about "open doors." We must not leave a door open for the enemy to enter. Please, put on the whole armor of God so that our bodies can be guarded, because unclean spirits come to try and destroy all of God's creations.

Chapter 12:
The Final Judgment

The Final Judgment on the Land:

Israel is at war right now against the Palestinians in 2024. We are living in the last days, where it is written about wars and rumors of wars and the final judgment of God's word. However, no one knows the day or the hour when Jesus will return. In Isaiah 44:24-27, it says:

(24) This is what the Lord says, your Redeemer and Creator: I am the Lord who made all things. I alone stretched out the heavens. Who was with me when I made the Earth?

(25) I expose false prophets as liars and make fools of fortune-tellers. I cause the wise to give bad advice, thus proving them to be fools.

(26) But I carry out the predictions of my prophets! By them, I say, 'Jerusalem's people will live here again, and the towns of Judah will be rebuilt. I will restore all your ruins.'

(27) When I speak to the rivers and say 'dry up,' they will dry up.

This is what's happening now—our rivers and oceans are drying up. In Isaiah 59:1-3, it continues:

(1) The Lord's arm is not too weak to save you, nor is his ear too deaf to hear you call.

(2) It's your sins that have cut you off from God. Because of your sins, he has turned away and will not listen anymore.

(3) Your hands are the hands of murderers, your fingers are filthy with sin, your lips are full of lies, and your mouth spews corruption.

To better understand God's judgment, continue reading Isaiah to learn how God will judge the world.

God said, "Do not add to or take away from my word, the Bible." No man, church, or organization has the right to remove the Book of Enoch or its scriptures, as some have done, portraying Enoch as a myth. Even Jude, the half-brother of Jesus, quoted Enoch's writings. Jude called Enoch a prophet and used his scriptures word for word. If Jude referred to Enoch as a prophet, and his writings were used, we too can trust and use them. If his writings were not considered scripture or divine, neither Jesus, Jude, nor Peter would have used them. The Book of Enoch is quoted over 112 times in the New Testament.

The church has had its day, and God's patience has run out for the churches. The apostles often wrote letters to correct them. The church has covered up the truth and taught false doctrines for hundreds of years. It is now too stubborn (or "gone") to change. All we can do is leave the churches, seek God's will, and meet in homes to restore what has been lost.

Genesis 6:4 speaks of how Noah warned the people of his time that the world must be punished for the sins of men and angels. He said the earth would be cleansed by the flood, and the angels would be imprisoned, cast into the earth until they are released during the Tribulation, as spoken about in the Book of Revelation.

I call this chapter "The Final Judgment on the Land" because God warned us in the Book of Revelation. The plagues are coming, and the seven-year Tribulation period is upon us.

There is a lot going on in the world today. Doctors are placing chips into people without their knowledge or permission. Breeding farms and human trafficking—especially sex trafficking—are prevalent in the United States. They show us these things on TV, but we don't pay attention to the truth of what's happening. Holy Scripture shows us what they are doing, but many aren't aware.

Judgment is upon the land, and this world system. The elites and Freemasons, who are the gatekeepers of this world system, are controlling what is happening and using God's word (the Bible) against God's chosen people. God said, "I'm bringing judgment upon this land because they took my people's land. They used and sold innocent children into prostitution."

The plagues that God is sending will be punishment for their actions (sins). God will judge His enemies—the people who scattered and oppressed His chosen ones. God said, "I will not let them get away with the abuse they have caused my people." We must pray and turn to God. We must gather the elders, children, and babies. God still has time. Give Him your heart and repent. We must cry out to God to spare us, so He can restore the land and save us.

Jeremiah 17:9-10 and Jeremiah 18:7-17 warn of what happens to those who refuse to return to God. We must be prepared for war. God said, "Tell my people the truth, and it will protect them from their enemies." Enoch spoke of scoffers—those who follow their own unnatural instincts, satisfying their ungodly desires. They do not have God's spirit in them.

God has the final say in our lives. He will not allow anyone to touch His chosen ones, His warriors. God will convict and bring judgment on this land and those who have spoken against Him.

God's judgment will come upon those who refuse to believe in Jesus. During these times, we must endure persecution, obey God's commandments, and keep our faith in Jesus. We must not focus on the natural world, but instead, look at what's happening spiritually and trust God. Anyone who worships the Beast and accepts the mark on their forehead or hand will feel God's anger and wrath. Judgment will fall on the land, and the seven angels will carry the plagues and the seven bowls of God's wrath. God is coming to punish the sinners and to destroy the Beast and those who have taken the mark of the Beast.

God's final judgment will come. We must remain faithful, trust in God, and be prepared, for He is coming like a thief in the night. People will begin to worship false gods and ignore the laws and commandments God placed in the Bible for His chosen people to live by.

The Battle of Armageddon:

Armageddon means "A place called Mount Megiddo," where good and evil will be fought. The hills of Megiddo are where the kings of the Earth, under demonic leaders, will wage war against the forces of God at the end of history. The Beast—a lion, an ox, a man, and an eagle—will be part of this final battle.

Megiddo is at the foot of Israel. It will be the site of the final battle of the end times before the coming of Christ (Yeshua). Babylon will be destroyed, but the end is not yet here. Yet wars, plagues, and natural disasters are signs of the Apocalypse—conquest, war, famine, and death.

The Plagues:

Painful Sores – Boils on the skin.

Water Turns to Blood – The sea becomes blood, killing everything in it.

Rivers and Springs – Water sources are corrupted.

Pain and Suffering – Afflicted upon those who worship the Beast.

Darkness Covers the Land – A deep, unnatural darkness falls.

The Drying Up of the Euphrates River – A sign of impending judgment.

The Battle of Armageddon – Mount Megiddo becomes a symbol of destruction and judgment. The end times have come, with earthquakes and plagues devastating the land.

Revelation 12:10:

"Then I heard a loud voice shouting across the heavens, 'It has come at last – salvation, power, and the Kingdom of God, and the authority of Jesus Christ!'"

The devil has come down to the land in great anger because his time on Earth is short. He is gathering as many souls as he can before his end. God says it is time for every knee to bow and every tongue to confess that He is Lord.

Repent and Pray – God has promised to heal the land if we turn to Him. Keep praying, for He hears our prayers.

These plagues are God's judgment. They come because of His anger, as punishments for the sins of the world. The Hebrew word mag ephah refers to a plague or slaughter – an illness or disease that will sweep across the land.

IT IS DONE……………………

Reference

Author Joseph B Lumpkin- The book of Enoch, The Angel, The watchers and the Nephilim.

Janet K Howard- Windowers of Delievence on spiritual Abuse.

NIV Bible, KIng James

Wikipedia.org